big & SMALL

Original Korean text by Bo-hyeon Seo
Illustrations by Jeong-hyeon Sohn
Korean edition © Aram Publishing

This English edition published by Big & Small in 2015
by arrangement with Aram Publishing
English text edited by Joy Cowley
English edition © Big & Small 2015

Distributed in the United States and Canada by
Lerner Publishing Group, Inc.
241 First Avenue North
Minneapolis, MN 55401 U.S. A.
www.lernerbooks.com

ISBN: 978-1-925186-15-4

Printed in Korea

What Shape Is the Moon?

Written by Bo-hyeon Seo
Illustrated by Jeong-hyeon Sohn
Edited by Joy Cowley

The owl sat in the tree and sang,
"Moon, moon, beautiful moon.
You are like a round ball
sitting on the top of the hill."

Just then, a fox came out of his cave.
"That song is wrong," said the fox.
"The moon is not a round ball."

"I saw the moon the other day,"
said the fox. "It was dented
and a bit flat on one side.
You should get your facts right."

A wild boar was passing by.
"You are both wrong," he said.
"The moon looks exactly like
half of a watermelon.
I saw it with my own eyes."

A bear came through the bushes.
"Half of a watermelon?
The moon is thin and curved
like a bent leaf. I know!
I saw it very clearly."

The little owl was confused.
"It was a round ball," she said.
"I'm sure I am right."

They all thought they were right about the shape of the moon.

I'm right!

No, I'm right!

19

While they were arguing,
a stork interrupted them.
"That's strange. I've seen every shape.
A dented moon, a half moon,
a curved moon and a full moon."

The other animals fell silent.

Finally, the little owl said,
"Why don't we wait
for the moon to rise.
Then we'll see who's right."

The others all agreed.
They climbed up the hill
to wait for the moon.

After a while, the moon came up.
It was round like a ball.

The owl flapped her wings.
"Look! I was right! I was right!"

The other animals were worried.

waxing crescent

first quarter

full moon

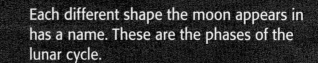

Each different shape the moon appears in has a name. These are the phases of the lunar cycle.

last quarter

waning crescent

The moon looked down and smiled.
"All the shapes you saw are mine.
They are made by the sun's light on me.
I'm round, but as the days pass by,
I appear to get smaller.
Later, you see me grow back,
little by little, to become full again."

"Thank you, Moon," said the animals,
and after that there were no arguments
about the shape of moon in the night sky.

What Shape Is the Moon?

The moon is a round sphere, like a ball.
It rises every evening but its shape seems
to change little by little, every night.

Let's think

Why does the moon appear to change shape?

Why isn't the moon seen during the day?

Why does the moon look spotty?

What are the phases of the lunar cycle?

Let's do!

Next time you are outside at nighttime, look for the moon.

Can you tell what phase in the lunar cycle it is?